CHRISTOPHER
and
CAROLINE
IN KENYA

JOANNE GRADY HUSKEY

Illustrated by Pixie Percival

To order additional copies of this book, contact:
Xlibris
844-714-8691
www.Xlibris.com
Orders@Xlibris.com

ISBN: Softcover   978-1-6698-2808-2
        EBook   978-1-6698-2807-5

Print information available on the last page

Rev. date: 06/16/2022

This book is dedicated to my children whose hearts are wide open to the world, and to their children, and to children everywhere who are curious and want to learn about people and cultures different from their own.

Christopher with his dark brown eyes was six years old, and his red-headed sister Caroline was three, when their Mommy and Daddy moved them to far off Africa. They were scared. What would Africa be like?

1

They flew to Kenya, a country right on the equator in the middle of our planet, where the sun rises at 6 am, and sets at 6 pm, every day, and the air is clean and cool.

Christopher and Caroline loved Kenya, because they had amazing adventures everyday. It is a place where the highlands are covered with green tea, and Mt. Kilimanjaro, the highest mountain in Africa, can be seen across the sky. It was a special place to grow up!

The garden of their house was filled with big banana and avocado trees. There, Caroline, in her big red rubber wellies, and Christopher in his many imaginative costumes were free to run and play outside all day with their dog, Jingle Bells, a golden cocker spaniel, who was their constant playmate.

Every morning, they could climb over their wall and meet their friends Willem and Mary, who loved to invent games and adventures.

On their land, was a fish pond full of golden carp, and a big swing that hung from an ancient tree, where they could fly to the treetops. Julia, their turtle, lived in their backyard under an arch of bougainvillea flowers that led to what they called their "secret garden."

Sometimes, in the early morning, Christopher would sneak outside into his garden before school to look at the amazing birds that were all around.

7

There were so many different kinds...hornbills, ibises, herons, egrets, kingfishers, spoonbills, green parrots and so many more.

Activity

Bird spotting is a great Kenya outdoor activity the whole family can enjoy, whether it's watching a Wagtail in the garden or a Bee-eater in the woods! Here are 18 birds for young spotters, ..how many do you know?

○ Superb Starling

○ Black Kyte

○ Maribu Stork

○ Hoopoe

○ Olive Trush

○ Weaver

○ Hummingbird

○ Bee-Eater

○ Firefinch

In Nairobi's National Park, there are over 650 bird species. Nairobi Game Park is a bird paradise! Nairobi has more bird species than any other capital city in the world. The Nairobi National Park's beautiful undisturbed grassland is very important for many species.

◯ Kingfisher

◯ Heron

◯ Mousebird

◯ Wagtail

◯ Green Parrot

◯ Hornbill

◯ Egret

◯ Spoonbill

◯ Ibis

In Kenya there are different tribes of people. The children's cook, Rose, was from the Kikuyu tribe; and Moses, their friendly gardener, was from the Luo tribe.

On the Maasai Mara, a big wide savannah, they could *see* people from the Maasai tribe, who wear red cloth and live on the land. All of them, however, are Kenyans. And even though the Kenyan flag shows a Maasai sword and two spears, the Kenyan people are very friendly and polite.

On weekends Caroline and Christopher would head out "on safari" with their parents. They'd stay in tents in the Maasai Mara and go out on the wide golden savannah in land rovers in the early mornings.

There, they could *see* lions, giraffes, zebras, wildebeests, warthogs, hyenas, rhinoceros, hippopotamus, and sometimes even cheetahs-- there was every kind of animal roaming in the morning sun.

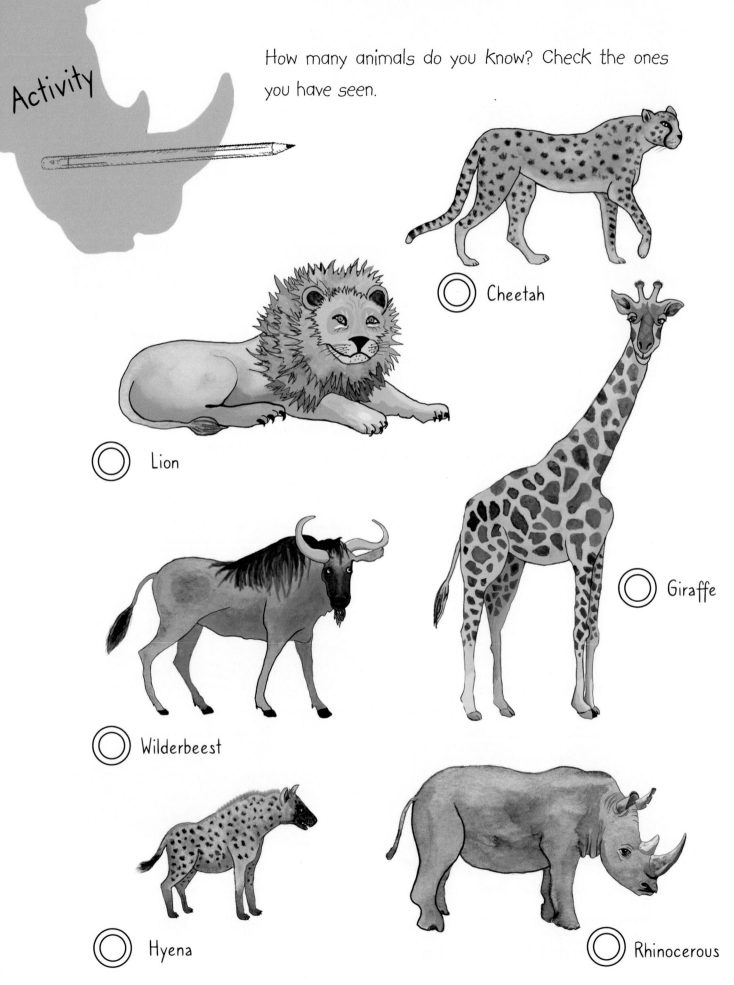

Activity

How many animals do you know? Check the ones you have seen.

⊙ Cheetah

⊙ Lion

⊙ Wilderbeest

⊙ Giraffe

⊙ Hyena

⊙ Rhinocerous

15

◯ Okapi

◯ Grants Gazelle

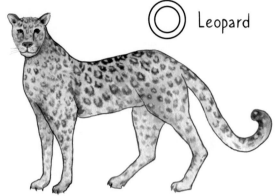

◯ Leopard

◯ Buffalo

◯ Hippopotamus

◯ Elephant

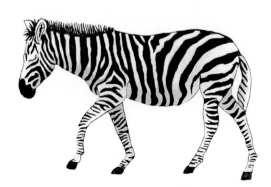

◯ Zebra

Other weekends they would go to Lake Nakuru where they could *see* hundreds of pink flamingos, or to Lake Naivasha, with loads of hippos lurking under the blue water.

Or, they might drive to the Great Rift Valley lined by dormant volcanoes, or go walking on Mount Kenya in the deep forest full of animals.

One time, Caroline and Christopher went to a place called il Ngwesi, which is a very special lodge run by Maasai warriors, carved into the side of a mountain deep in the wilderness. Their room had no walls and an outdoor shower, where they could yell into the forest and their voices rang out for miles.

In the early morning, they went on a safari sitting high on camels, and tall Maasai warriors cooked their breakfast over a fire in the bush.

Once in a while, they would go to the coast of Kenya to the white beach in the town of Malindi, or to the Island of Lamu. Lamu is an island of Muslim people, where the women cover their hair and wear long dark robes.

There are no cars on the island, so donkeys carry people through the small lanes lined with white houses. Big sail boats, called dhows, flash their huge white sails around the seacoast.

Growing up in Kenya was enchanting for Christopher and Caroline. They loved learning all about the many Kenyan tribes, and seeing the amazing diversity of animals and birds. They especially loved their days of freedom playing in the yellow African sunlight covering the land.

For Christopher and Caroline, Africa was a magical place that changed their lives. Maybe one day you, too, will go to Africa, or meet someone who is African and that enchanting far away land will change your life!

Christopher and Caroline when they lived in Kenya

Christopher and Caroline today.

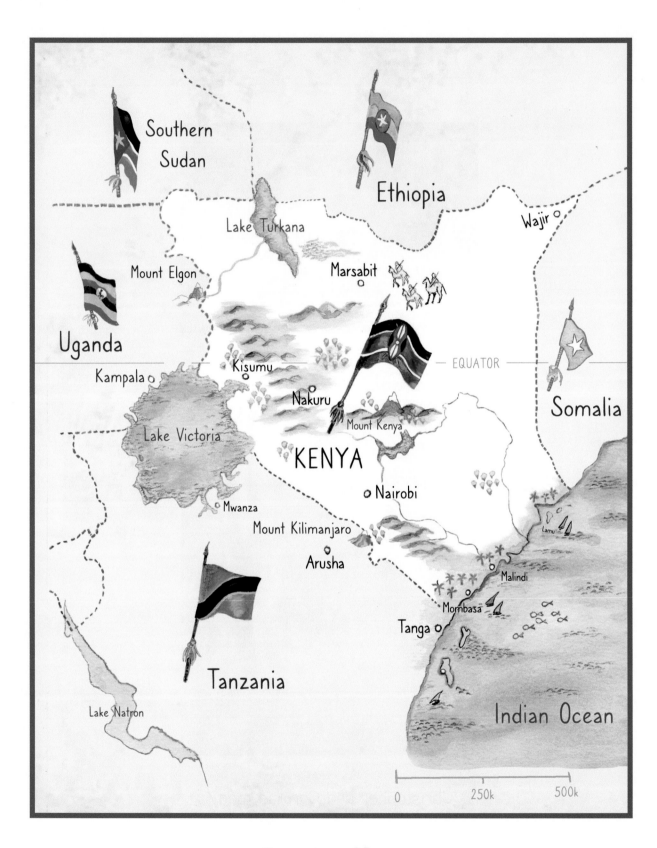

Country Map

About the Author

Joanne Grady Huskey is a cross cultural trainer and educator who has traveled widely and dedicated her life to promoting understanding between people of diverse cultures. Her work has taken her to every continent. Having lived in Kenya for three years,she has a lifelong love for that country. In this book she hopes to excite children with dreams of other lands, in the hope that it will be the beginning of a lifetime of discovery and openness to the world.

About the Illustrator

Pixie Percival has spent over 30 years in Africa. She draws her artistic inspiration from her time in Nigeria and then Kenya. For many years Pixie has been interested in illustrating stories and specializes in mythology and narratives from Africa. Working in mixed media, with gouache, watercolor and pencil. Pixie holds a Bachelor of Arts degree in illustration from the University of Herefordshire, along with diplomas in Botanical Painting and Humanities.

Printed in the United States
by Baker & Taylor Publisher Services